my little Pony

little Pony

Contents

Pedigree®

Published by Pedigree Books Limited
Beech Hill House, Walnut Gardens, Exeter, Devon EX4 4DH.
E-mail books@pedigreegroup.co.uk
Published 2004

My Little Pony and all related characters are trademarks
of Hasbro & are used with permission.

Licensing by:

Hasbro
Properties
Group

£6.99

Meet the Ponies

Pinkie Pie

Pinkie Pie is the sweetest lamb of a Pony who loves trying new, fun things, but sometimes she gets just a little bit nervous.

Kimono

Kimono is the most wise knowing Pony in all of Ponyland. Kimono tells of times past, like when the forests were filled with beautiful Unicorns.

Minty

Did you know that Minty collects socks? No one in Ponyland even wears socks let alone collects them! No one, that is, except Minty

Sweetberry

Sweetberry can whip up a Cocoa Mocha Rainbowberry Peanut Butter Float or a Key Lime Blueberry Liquorice Pie like no one else can! You're going to have a blast with Sweetberry.

Sparkleworks

Have you ever flown over Ponyland in a hot air balloon? You haven't? Then you need to go for a ride with Sparkleworks.

Rainbow Dash

Rainbow Dash is the most outrageous Pony you'll ever meet! When it comes to adventure, excitement and fun, if Rainbow Dash hasn't done it, it's never been done!

Sunny Daze

The very first time you meet Sunny Daze, watch out! She's so friendly, she'll nearly bowl you over running right up to you and giggling, "Hi! Want to play?"

Wysteria

Wysteria is the best listener in all of Ponyland. She is gentle and kind and loves to surprise her friends!

PONY COLOUR MATCH

Pinkie Pie and Kimono are having fun playing together.
You can have fun colouring the picture the same way
or making up your own colours.

9

Pair The Pony Shadow

Rainbow Dash, Kimono and Pinkie Pie have all lost their shadows, help them find them by drawing a line from the pony to her matching shadow

SPOT THE DIFFERENCE

Match the Pose

Sweetberry looks good in any pose.
Can you see which two poses are exactly the same.

A

B

C

D

E

"All right, everyone – time to get off! We're here!" shouts the driver. Everyone is so excited!

"Stay in a group and don't go too far!" warns the teacher.

The ponies set off walking, looking at everything around them: the fallen leaves, the toadstools...

"Oh, look! A squirrel!"

The Little Ponies seem amazed by the woodland world. Only Sweetberry is lagging behind. She has spotted something more interesting than what the teacher is talking about.

"Mmm, yummy!" she says. "These blackberries are delicious!"

While her friends walk further ahead, Sweetberry disappears into the woods in search of more berries...until she realises she cannot see anyone else.

"Where are they?" she says to herself. "They could have waited for me! Oh, dear! How am I going to find them again?"

Oh, no! Sweetberry is completely lost! Worried, she sits down and begins to cry.

"I must be brave," she sniffs. "I should be all right if I retrace my steps..."

That is just what she does. Sweetberry walks and walks...but the further she goes, the more unfamiliar her surroundings become. Seeing a handkerchief that she has dropped, she realises that she has gone round in a circle!

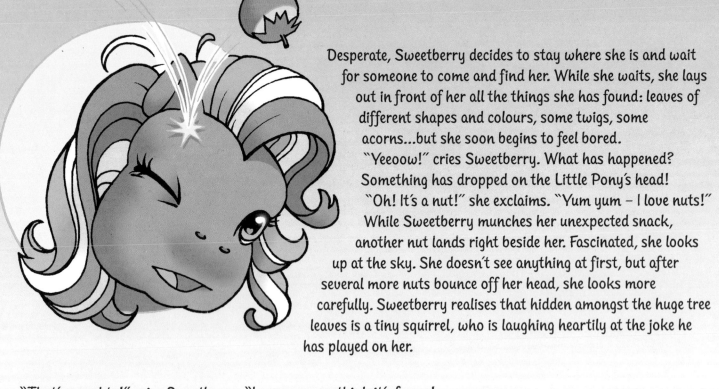

Desperate, Sweetberry decides to stay where she is and wait for someone to come and find her. While she waits, she lays out in front of her all the things she has found: leaves of different shapes and colours, some twigs, some acorns...but she soon begins to feel bored.
"Yeeoow!" cries Sweetberry. What has happened? Something has dropped on the Little Pony's head!
"Oh! It's a nut!" she exclaims. "Yum yum – I love nuts!" While Sweetberry munches her unexpected snack, another nut lands right beside her. Fascinated, she looks up at the sky. She doesn't see anything at first, but after several more nuts bounce off her head, she looks more carefully. Sweetberry realises that hidden amongst the huge tree leaves is a tiny squirrel, who is laughing heartily at the joke he has played on her.

"That's naughty!" cries Sweetberry. "I suppose you think it's funny! Wait, don't go..."
But it begins to pour with rain and the squirrel disappears into the trees. Sweetberry is wondering where to shelter when she spots an enormous old tree nearby that has an opening in its trunk.
"Wow!" she exclaims. "That's almost as big as a house!"

Sweetberry didn't know how right she was: inside the tree is a family of rabbits – Daddy Rabbit, Mummy Rabbit and their four kittens. All six of them are frightened of Sweetberry. The little rabbits have never met a Little Pony before. Sweetberry tries to reassure them:
"Don't be scared!" she says. "I don't mean any harm!"

Our little friend tells them the story of how she came to be lost in the woods. Having listened intently, Daddy Rabbit comes over and says in his little voice:
"I can help you to find your way back, if you agree to help us, too."
"Oh, of course I will," Sweetberry smiles. "What can I do for you?"
"Well, we are from a big city and we are going to stay with our cousin in the country. We still have a long way to go and our children are very tired -they're still only babies. If you take us on your back, that would be much quicker!"

Without hesitating for a second, Sweetberry helps her new friends on to her back. Following Daddy Rabbit's directions, she gallops to the edge of the woods, where she finds the other Little Ponies again.

"Oh, look! It's Sweetberry!" they cry.

"But where have you been?" asks the teacher. "We've been looking for you everywhere!"

"It's a long story," Sweetberry replies, a little out of breath.

"Come on! Everyone on the bus!"

"I'm coming! But first...um...I have something to do..."

Sweetberry races off out of sight to a nearby field to drop off the Rabbit family.

"There you are. Now we can go our separate ways," she smiles. "Good luck with the rest of your journey!"

"Goodbye, little Sweetberry! Hee, hee, hee!" giggle the rabbits.

And so, this is a story with a happy ending: Sweetberry found her way back safely and she also made some new friends. One thing is certain: none of it would have happened had she not loved her food so much!

The Perfect Pony

Take all the best bits of your favourite ponies or create your own designs, then draw them on the silhouette below to create your perfect pony.

The Enchanted Mask

Sunny Daze loves rummaging through the castle attic. She always finds something interesting there. One Sunday afternoon, she decides to take Rainbow Dash, Minty and Wisteria, her three best friends, to her special place.

"Where are we going?" asks Minty.

"It's a surprise!"

"Oh! I know this place: it's the castle!" grumbles Rainbow Dash. "Is that your surprise?"

"Shush! Follow me..."

The friends follow the staircase to the top, where Sunny Daze explains that they will have to go up a ladder to get to the attic.

"Come on! Be brave!"

"It's too high!" complains Minty. "I should have stayed with Sweetberry to try her sardine and jam cakes with delicious hot chocolate and cinnamon...

"Don't be silly! We're going to have some fun!" Sunny Daze says eagerly. She is the only one, though, who can see what's so good about this little expedition...

At the top, the ponies suddenly come to an impressive door. There seems to be a strange atmosphere in this part of the castle... Sunny Daze pushes the huge door and invites Rainbow Dash, Minty and Wisteria to follow her in. A little anxious, they go in on tiptoe, huddling together.

"Aaa...atchoo! It's really dusty in here!"

"Huh! There's just piles of old stuff – let's go!" says Wisteria.

Suddenly, Minty comes across a marvellous book. A book? Sunny Daze has never seen it before.

"Let me see! It's called The Book of..."

"Hmm...I can't quite read it..."

"...of Mysteries!"

"The Book of Mysteries? But what is it?" Could it be a book of magic? Wisteria opens it and begins to read while Minty and Rainbow Dash go over to a trunk full of costumes.

"Oh! Look at this mask! It's lovely!" While they look at what they've found, Wisteria carries on trying to make out what is written in the old book.

Putting on a serious voice, she reads out the strange words: "Arali trouverus que li mascus...oh, I don't understand any of it at all!"

"It doesn't matter," whispers Minty, "carry on!"

"Practis etteram...Plum! Zazarius..."

What is happening? Rainbow Dash is pointing frantically to the trunk.

"The mask! The mask moved!" she cries.

"Artific nactea..." Sunny Daze continues.

FZZZZZZZZZZZZZZZZZZZZ!

Suddenly, the mask flies through the air like an arrow, damaging any furniture or clothes in its path. To escape this whirlwind, the Little Ponies run and hide in a wardrobe. Gradually, silence returns. When they peep out of their hiding place, the mask has disappeared. In a panic, they run out of the attic and down the staircase. But at the bottom, they get a shock: the mask has ransacked the castle!

With a blanket in her hand, Minty jumps on the mask and manages to catch it. The ponies feel relieved and the mask seems calm.

"This mask is so strange!" says Minty. "Two minutes ago, it was going mad and now it's an ordinary mask again!"

Kimono comes in and interrupts her friends:
"It's not that ordinary! Look what I found in the library archives!"
While she was looking for information on the Ponyville Grand Carnival, Kimono has found an old newspaper that tells the strange story of an enchanted mask...
"Let me see the mask, Minty," says Kimono.

There is no doubt: the mask in the Ponyville newspaper looks just like the one from the attic! The story says that the mask is enchanted; it has magic powers and those who have worn it have mysteriously disappeared for several days, before waking up in their own bed remembering nothing of what has happened.
"That's all very mysterious," says Minty. "I'd like to try that mask on."
"You're mad!" exclaims Sunny Daze. "What if you disappear forever?"
But Minty has already put the mask on.
"Hey, that mask suits you! You look like a princess - go and have a look in the mirror!"
Suddenly, Minty begins to feel strange and, little by little, disappears.
"Oh, but...what's happening to me? Goodb-"

Minty wakes up to see Kimono holding a sports trophy.

"That's funny – Kimono doesn't like sport," she thinks.

Then Sunny Daze comes in, carrying a delicious bacon and banana cake drizzled with strawberry mint juice.

"Very strange," Minty says to herself.

"It's usually Sweetberry who cooks us nice snacks..."

Now Sweetberry appears, wearing spectacles and reading a book.

"But...Kimono's the one who normally reads stories!"

Rainbow Dash, who loves sliding down rainbows, is picking up socks!

"This is a topsy-turvy world!" thinks Minty, in a panic. "Hey, everyone! Is this your idea of a joke?"

Minty tries to speak but no one seems to see or hear her. It is as if she has become a ghost...

When Minty wakes up in her bed, her friends are round her.

"Well?" asks Kimono.

"Well what?" Minty replies. "Why is there a mask in my hand?"

Minty has forgotten her journey to the land of dreams, and the mystery of the enchanted mask will remain a mystery forever. That same evening, Sunny Daze takes the mask back up to the attic and buries it at the bottom of the trunk. She sticks a label to it that says: `Beware! This mask is enchanted!´

Who knows? Maybe one day, another curious Little Pony will discover the mystery of the magic mask!

In trying to be too clever, Minty tumbles from the ladder and lands on the bag of Christmas baubles.

"Oh, well done! Now the baubles are all broken!" scolds Kimono.

"We'll never be ready in time!" wails Rainbow Dash, seeing garlands fall from the ceiling and needles beginning to drop from the tree.

Our little friends are not really cut out for putting up decorations. What a disaster! All their efforts have been wasted. The Little Ponies are crestfallen. Pinky Pie and Kimono decide to go for a walk and have a rethink.

"There's something shining over there!" exclaims Pinky Pie.

"Oh! What is it? Let's go and see," suggests Kimono.

The two friends head off towards the strange light...they run like lightning, the wind in their manes, across the snow-covered fields of Ponyville. As they get nearer, the light gets bigger and leads them to a clearing just beyond the lavender hill.

"You go first," says Kimono.

"No, you! You're the bravest one," Pinky Pie replies.

Kimono walks on slowly, but trips on a stone and goes somersaulting down to the bottom of the hill.

"I've just found the most amazing thing!" she cries.

It's a star! A twinkling star, on a sparkling wand! Incredible though it may seem, the wand begins to dance and twirl in the sky, leaving a shimmering trail of gold, silver, pink and blue stars. Kimono looks on, transfixed, and is soon joined by Pinky Pie.

"All those lights...they're beautiful!" gasps Pinky Pie.

"It's magical!" agrees Kimono. "Do you think I could make a wish? I wish I could fly!"

As soon as she has said it, the wand begins to glow brightly and Kimono is magically whisked up in a swirl of stars...

Pinky Pie and Kimono realise that the wand is magic and that it could make all their wishes come true. The two friends decide to take it back with them so that it can help them decorate the castle...

The little wand is so pleased to have made new friends that it lights up everything in its path and leaves thousands of stars behind it, each more beautiful than the last. Ponyville is covered in shimmering lights and the Little Ponies are delighted.

Pinky Pie and Kimono arrive at the castle and see that no more decorations have been put up. Things have even got worse: the garlands are torn and the baubles are smashed; Sunny Daze and Rainbow Dash are squabbling; Sparkleworks and Sweetberry have given up and are eating the cakes meant for the party. Drastic action is needed if the Christmas party is to take place as planned...

"I've got a surprise for you," says Kimono.
"Oh, yes? Have you got the magic formula to get the castle decorated in the blink of an eye?" asks Minty.
"And why not?" smiles Kimono, holding up the wand.
"This is a magic wand," Pinky Pie adds, "and it can help us! Can't you, little wand?"
Suddenly, the beautiful star begins to glow very brightly...and to spin all round the room.
"Look at all those wonderful stars!" gasps Rainbow Dash.
Everyone is smiling again. Wisteria puts on some music and the Little Ponies dance around wildly, singing at the top of their voices.
"La la la...tra la la la la!

The garlands twirl in the air, back into place; the baubles that are scattered on the floor are magically hung on the tree. Kimono, who didn't know how she would put up the star, begins to fly to the top of the tree with it. Everything is now easy: all they have to do is wish for what they want. The castle is gradually transformed into a fairytale palace, showered with shimmering stars and beautiful decorations...

The dancing Little Ponies are enjoying themselves so much, none of them notices that the wand has disappeared. It is Sweetberry, coming from the kitchen with her delicious freshly-baked cakes, who realises.

"Hey, everyone! Where's the magic wand?"

Sunny Daze, Pinky Pie, Rainbow Dash and Minty look around them and, realising that the wand has vanished, forget to watch what they're doing and fall over each other.

"But there'll be no more magic now! Oh! Watch out!"

Luckily, the ponies don't hurt themselves. Just the opposite: they laugh at what has happened.

"Ha, ha, ha! Oops a-daisy!" giggles Minty.

The Christmas party was a great success, after all. As for the little wand, no one in Ponyville ever saw it again. But our little friends will never forget it. Sweetberry even made up a recipe in its honour: Christmas Star Biscuits!

53

57

All the girls are here ready for you to brighten up their days with a little colour.